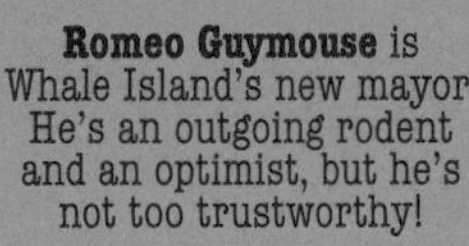
Romeo Guymouse is Whale Island's new mayor. He's an outgoing rodent and an optimist, but he's not too trustworthy!

Gary is an Australian surfing champion! Shy and reserved, he's only at ease on the ocean waves! He'll never desert his surfboard, "Stella."

Thea Stilton

PAPERCUTZ™

Thea Stilton

Graphic Novels Available from PAPERCUTZ™

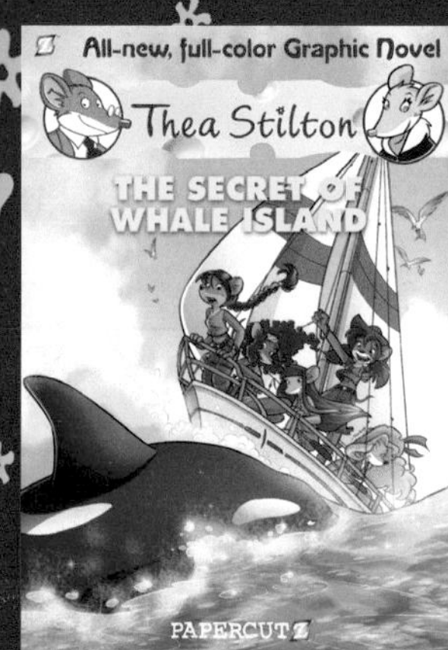

Graphic Novel #1
"The Secret of Whale Island"

Graphic Novel #2
"Revenge of the Lizard Club"

Graphic Novel #3
"The Treasure of the Viking Ship"

Graphic Novel #4
"Catching the Giant Wave"

THEA STILTON graphic novels are available for $9.99 each only in hardcover. Available from booksellers everywhere. You can also order online from www.papercutz.com. Or call 1-800-886-1223, Monday through Friday, 9 – 5 EST. MC, Visa, and AmEx accepted. To order by mail, please add $4.00 for postage and handling for first book ordered, $1.00 for each additional book and make check payable to NBM Publishing. Send to: Papercutz, 160 Broadway, Suite 700, East Wing, New York, NY 10038.

THEA STILTON graphic novels are also available digitally wherever e-books are sold.

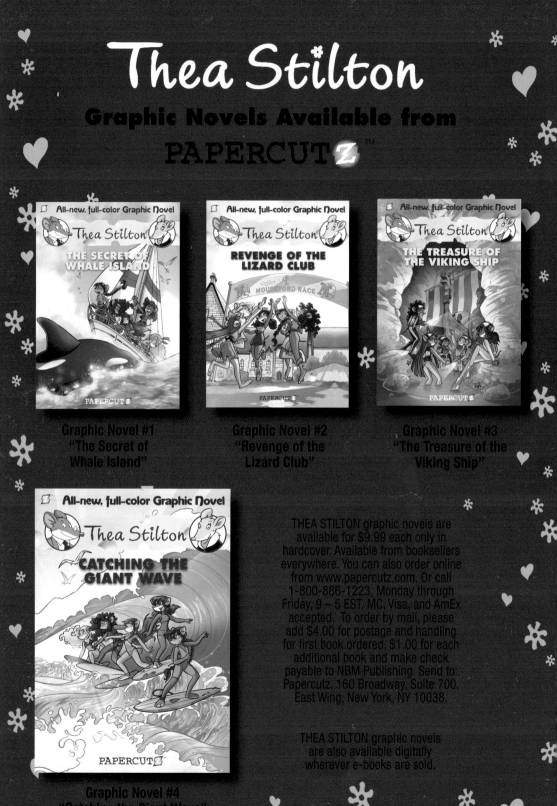

Thea Stilton

CATCHING THE GIANT WAVE

By Thea Stilton

PAPERCUTZ™
New York

THEA STILTON #4
CATCHING THE GIANT WAVE

Text by Thea Stilton
Text Coordination by Sarah Rossi (Atlantyca S.p.A.)
Editorial Coordination by Patrizia Puricelli and Serena Bellani
Artistic Coordination by Flavio Ferron
With the assistance of Tommaso Valsechi
Editing by Yellowhale
Editing Coordination and Artwork Supervision by Stefania Bitta and Maryam Funicelli
Script Supervision by Francesco Artibani
Story by Francesco Artibani and Caterina Mognato
Design by Arianna Rea
Art by Michela Frare
Color by Ketty Formaggio
With the assistance of Marta Lorini
Cover by Arianna Rea (design), Michela Frare (art), and Ketty Formaggio (color)

Based on an original idea by Elisabetta Dami

Original title: "Aspettando L'onda Gigante"
Translation by: Nanette McGuinness
www.geronimostilton.com

Lettering & Production – Big Bird Zatryb
Production Coordinator – Beth Scorzato
Editor – Robyn Chapman
Associate Editor – Michael Petranek
Editor-in-Chief
Jim Salicrup

ISBN: 978-1-62991-050-5

Printed in China.
September 2014 by WKT Co. LTD.
3/F Phase 1 Leader Industrial Centre
188 Texaco Road, Tsuen Wan, N.T.
Hong Kong

Distributed by Macmillan
First Papercutz Printing

FINALLY A LOVELY DAY OF SUN ON Whale Island! NICKY JUMPS AT THE CHANCE TO TEACH PAMELA AND PAULINA HOW TO SURF.
THE ROUGH, CHOPPY SEA AT VERY WINDY POINT CALLS TO HER IRRESISTIBLY-- SINCE SHE'S USED TO THE OCEAN WAVES OF AUSTRALIA!
DON'T STIFFEN UP, PAM! LOOSE LEGS AND AN IRON WILL!
PULVERIZED PISTONS!
LOOK, VIOLET! PAM'S FACING HER FIRST WAVE!
EEEH-- GLUB!
FWOOSH
SPLUT!
HA! HA! HA! YOU LOOK LIKE A SEAL, PAM! HEE! HEE!

CREE-
CREE-
CREE
HANG IN THERE, PAM! YOU'VE GOT A FUTURE-- AHEM IN THE FUNNY PAGES! HA! HA!
HUFF EVEN YOU'VE GOT SURF FEVER!
ZIP
GULP!
MARY SQUID* HAS SUDDENLY POPPED OUT LIKE A FURY!
WHAT'LL BECOME OF MY BURROS, HEY? WHERE'RE THEY GOING TO FIND A LITTLE PEACE FROM NOW ON?
* ONE OF DINA'S SISTERS. SHE RAISES BURROS AND LIKES TO DANCE.
??
THEY'RE DELICATE, GENTLE ANIMALS... NOISE STRESSES THEM! THEY'RE TIMID, SHRINKING FLOWERS, REALLY!
I DIDN'T THINK WE WERE SHOUTING THAT LOUDLY!
CALM DOWN, FRILLY!
THEY WON'T BE ABLE TO STAND AN INVASION OF THOUSANDS OF TOURISTS, JEEPS, AND STINKY, NOISY MOTORBOATS!
BUT THERE'RE JUST FIVE OF US... AND WE CAME ON FOOT!
YES, BUT HOW MANY OF YOU WILL THERE BE WHEN THEY BUILD THE SURF CENTER? RUINING SUCH A BEAUTIFUL BEACH FOR A SILLY SPORT!
WHO WANTS TO BUILD A SURF CENTER?

MARY HEARD ABOUT THE NEW CENTER FROM HER SISTER DINA. SO THE THEA SISTERS DECIDE TO GET THE EXPLANATION STRAIGHT FROM HER...
IT'S THE MAYOR'S INITIATIVE! HE WANTS TO COMPETE WITH VISSIA DE VISSEN AND HER SURF CLUB.
REALLY?!
I DON'T EVEN KNOW WHO THE MAYOR IS...
THEY JUST ELECTED HIM! IT'S ROMEO, VINCE GUYMOUSE'S COUSIN!
OH, THE OWNER OF THE RESTAURANT "CHEZ ROMEO!"
REALLY A NICE FUTURE!
THE OLD CITY COUNCIL WAS AN OUTDATED INSTITUTION! THE ISLAND NEEDS A MODERN ADMINISTRATION!
ROMEO EXAGGERATES, BUT HE'S NOT BAD.
BUT WHY ELECT HIM, PRECISELY?
NO ONE ELSE WANTED TO TAKE ON THE JOB!
ROMEO'S TRAVELLED THE WORLD! HE'S SEEN HOW THINGS WORK ELSEWHERE! AND NOW THAT HE'S BACK, HE WANTS TO "LAUNCH OUR ISLAND INTO THE FUTURE!"... OR AT LEAST THAT'S WHAT HE SAYS...
"ROMEO GUYMOUSE IS A MAYOR WITH LOTS OF IDEAS AND INITIATIVES!"
WE'LL TRANSFORM WHALE ISLAND INTO A PARADISE FOR THE RICH FROM AROUND THE WORLD!
IF ONLY RICH FOLKS STAY HERE, WHERE'LL OUR FISHERMEN GO?
EXCLUSIVE HOTELS! ADVANCED TECHNOLOGY! VERY DISTINGUISHED CLIENTELE!

YOU'LL GET RICH, TOO! IT'LL BE LIKE LIVING IN THE LAND OF PLENTY, DEVON, YOU'LL SEE!
I'VE ALWAYS EARNED MY OWN CHEESE! NO ONE'S EVER GIVEN ME ANYTHING!
THINGS'LL CHANGE, MY FRIEND! I'LL SHOW YOU-- LET ME TREAT ALL OF YOU AT MY RESTAURANT!
Chez Romeo
HURRAY FOR MY COUSIN!
BRAVO FOR THE MAYOR!
WHEN'LL YOU GIVE US ALL LUNCH, TOO, ROMEO?
I'LL STAY FOR A MINUTE, BUT EATING AT HIS PLACE? YUCK!
ROMEO'S NOT A BAD RODENT AT HEART!
HE'S JUST A BIT TOO MUCH OF, HOW SHOULD I SAY IT... AN OPTIMIST AND A DREAMER!
BUT EVEN ROMEO GUYMOUSE HAS HIS PROBLEMS!
MY RESTAURANT IS VERY BEAUTIFUL BUT... IT'S ALWAYS EMPTY!
MMM... HER CHEESE CANAPÉS GO RIGHT TO MY HEART!
I CAN'T FIND A COOK WHO MEASURES UP! AH, IF ONLY MIDGE WORKED FOR ME...

QUICK, KID, GO TO THE FLORIST RIGHT AWAY! BUY A BUNCH OF ROSES AND SEND THEM TO MOUSEFORD ACADEMY... TO MISS MIDGE, FROM ME!
-GULP!- YES, SIR!
HEY! WHO WANTS TO ASK FOR THE HAND OF YOUR DAUGHTER MIDGE?
-HMPH!-
VISSIA DE VISSEN'S DREAMS ARE MUCH MORE PRACTICAL THAN ROMEO'S...
MY SURF CLUB OPENS IN A WEEK! THE MOST LUXURIOUS IN THE WORLD!
AND THIS IS JUST THE BEGINNING! NOW IT'S TIME TO EXPAND MY RANGE OF OPERATIONS!
WELCOME, MR. MAYOR!

WHAT'S THE MAYOR DOING ON VISSIA'S YACHT?
SO, MY DEAR ROMEO, WILL THERE BE A SURF CENTER ON DONKEY BEACH OR NOT?
MY FELLOW CITIZENS ARE TRADITIONALISTS. PROJECTS LIKE THIS ALARM THEM! I DON'T KNOW IF...
TSK! STILL HESITATING?!
I JUST SHELLED OUT BILLIONS TO MAKE WINDY ISLAND INTO THE MOST EXCLUSIVE, SURFING-EST RESORT IN THE WORLD!
I EVEN HAD A REEF BUILT SO THE WAVES WILL BE PERFECT YEAR ROUND!
COUGH! COUGH! THERE'LL BE ONE! COUGH! THERE'LL BE ONE...
BUT MY ISLAND WILL ONLY HOUSE A FEW PRIVILEGED PEOPLE! MASS TOURISM IS WHAT WILL BRING IN BIG PROFITS!
THAT'S WHY I WANT YOU TO BUILD A SURF CENTER ON WHALE ISLAND! TO HOUSE THE CROWDS OF TOURISTS... WHO WILL BRING IN SO MUCH MONEY!
YES. AHEM... OF COURSE!
I HAD MY EXPERTS DRAW UP PLANS!
ALAN, THE SLIDES!
FIRST, WE'LL CONSTRUCT AN ARTIFICIAL REEF HERE, TOO!
SECOND, WE'LL CREATE A BIG... NO, A HUGE HOTEL ON RAM PLAIN!

THIRD, WE'LL BUILD SEASIDE FACILITIES ON DONKEY BEACH!
CLAP CLAP CLAP
SPLENDID!

BUT... APPROVAL OF A PROJECT LIKE THIS REQUIRES A POPULAR REFERENDUM...
WELL? THEN HAVE ONE RIGHT AWAY!

WITH MY MONEY, YOU'LL BE SURE TO WIN!
WHALE ISLAND'S RESIDENTS WOULD NEVER ALLOW A STRANGER TO PUT HER PAWS IN THEIR ISLAND'S BUSINESS!

OUR AGREEMENT WILL REMAIN SECRET, OF COURSE!
IT'S BETTER THAT WAY! I'VE MADE IT SEEM THAT THE SURF CENTER IS MY IDEA... TO GIVE YOU COMPETITION!

PERFECT! HA! HA! HA!

NEWS OF WHALE ISLAND'S SURF CENTER REFERENDUM EVEN REACHED MOUSEFORD ACADEMY!
WE ALSO WANT TO BUILD A SURF CENTER ON WHALE ISLAND...
HEE! HEE! HEE!
HEH! HEH!
?

... BUT ALL THE VIPS WILL BE AT MY MOTHER'S CENTER, ON WINDY ISLAND!
ALL... EXCEPT FOR THE REAL SURFING CHAMPIONS!

YOU'RE WRONG! DO YOU KNOW WHO'S GOING TO OPEN THE SURF CLUB? NONE OTHER THAN GARY MOON!

THEY'RE EVEN GOING TO FILM COMMERCIALS... WITH JUST GARY AND ME!
HEE! HEE! HEE!

MOM'S PUBLICISTS DECIDED! AND HE'S GOING TO FALL IN LOVE WITH ME!
OH! HOW ROMANTIC!
GARY'S SO CUTE!
PHOOEY! WHO IS GARY MOON? HA! HA!

HEY?! WHAT'S GOTTEN INTO YOU? AND WHAT'S UP WITH NICKY?
GARY MOON'S THE AUSTRALIAN SURFING CHAMPION! NICKY'S OBSESSED WITH HIM... DIDN'T YOU KNOW?
SMAK
OH, NOW I GET IT! HE'S THE GUY ON THE POSTER IN HER ROOM!
WHAT AN AWFUL BLOW, TO FIND OUT HE'LL BE VANILLA'S GUEST. POOR NICKY!
WHY WOULD GARY CARE ABOUT A FLIRT LIKE VANILLA?
WOW! HE'S REALLY CUTE!
DO YOU WANT ME TO GET HIS AUTOGRAPH, NICKY?
OH, PAM, THAT WOULD BE FANTASTIC!
LEAVE IT TO AN EXPERT! YOU'LL SEE. I'LL EVEN MANAGE TO GET YOU A DEDICATION!

AND THE REFERENDUM? DID YOU FORGET ABOUT IT, KIDS? WE'VE GOT TO SEE THAT THE MAYOR'S PLAN DOESN'T PASS!
RIGHT! BUT, HOW?
LET'S ASK THE HEADMASTER...!
SO, A LITTLE LATER...
I SHARE YOUR CONCERNS, KIDS, BUT MOUSEFORD ACADEMY'S CHARTER DOESN'T ALLOW US TO INTERFERE WITH ISLAND POLITICS!
OH...
YOU'RE SO WELL RESPECTED ON THE ISLAND...
I'M SORRY, BUT MY PAWS ARE TIED!
SO, WHO CAN HELP US NOW?
PROFESSOR VAN KRAKEN WILL CERTAINLY LEND US A PAW!
YES, BUT HIS LANGUAGE IS TOO... TECHNICAL.
YOU MEAN, NO ONE CAN UNDERSTAND HIM!
ROMEO GUYMOUSE, ON THE OTHER HAND, SURE KNOWS HOW TO GET PEOPLE TO LISTEN!
YOU'RE RIGHT! OUR MAYOR'S A GREAT SPEAKER!
AND HE'S SO DISTINGUISHED! A REAL GENTLEMOUSE!
I'M AFRAID THE BATTLE IS LOST BEFORE WE START...
NO, NO, AND ONCE AGAIN, NO! OUR BATTLE ISN'T LOST. OUR BATTLE IS RIGHTEOUS!

"AGREED. PROFESSOR VAN KRAKEN ISN'T A GREAT SPEAKER, BUT HE CAN ALWAYS LEND US A PAW."

I'M WITH YOU, KIDS!

FIRST OF ALL, LET'S GO SEE WHAT MS. DE VISSEN HAS DONE TO THE SEA FLOOR.

ENCLOSED SPACES AREN'T SO GOOD FOR ME... THE LAST TIME WAS TORTURE...

THERE'S NO OTHER WAY TO INSPECT THE ARTIFICIAL REEF.

UMM... THE SUBMERSIBLE IS SO TINY AND I...

DON'T WORRY, NICKY! WE DON'T ALL NEED TO GO!

I'LL STAY ON DRY LAND WITH YOU!

I DON'T WANT TO GO UNDERWATER EITHER. THE HUMIDITY WILL MAKE MY HAIR ALL FRIZZY!

TAKE THE KEY TO MY ATV! GO SEE WHAT'S HAPPENING IN TOWN!

LOOK AT ALL THOSE POSTERS!
WHERE'D HE FIND THE MONEY FOR A CAMPAIGN LIKE THIS?
I'M LOOKING INTO THE FUTURE
YOU KNOW WHAT I SAY? I SMELL A RAT HERE!
THERE WAS NO LACK OF SURPRISES UNDERWATER, EITHER!
THE REEF IS GIGANTIC!
WHAT'S THAT THING MADE OF, PROFESSOR?
THEY'RE ENORMOUS SACKS OF SAND, PAM! BUT IT'S TOO BIG. I CAN'T FIGURE OUT ITS EXACT CONFIGURATION.
WE COULD TAKE PICTURES OF IT AND MEASURE IT!
YOU'RE RIGHT, PAULINA! THAT WILL SERVE AS ACCURATE DOCUMENTATION! THEN I'LL CONTACT SOME EXPERTS ABOUT IT!

THAT EVENING, AFTER RETURNING FROM THEIR RESPECTIVE "MISSIONS," THE THEA SISTERS WERE SUMMONED TO THE ACADEMY'S GREAT HALL, ALONG WITH ALL THE OTHER STUDENTS...
HERE'S A NICE ANNOUNCEMENT! WE'VE BEEN INVITED TO MS. DE VISSEN'S FOR THE OPENING OF THE SURF CLUB ON WINDY ISLAND!
THE FESTIVITIES WILL LAST THE ENTIRE WEEKEND!
YEAH!
HURRAY FOR VANILLA!
HURRAY FOR VIC!
HI, VIC! UM... CAN I TALK TO YOU?
TALK TO ME? WHAT AN HONOR, MISS PAMELA!
I'D LIKE TO ASK A FAVOR OF YOU... UM, IF I MIGHT!
SOMETHING SECRET?! I'M INTRIGUED. SPIT IT OUT!
OH, FOR HEAVEN'S SAKE! NICKY ADORES SURFING AND IS A FAN OF GARY MOON... PERHAPS YOU COULD...
... TEAR HIM OUT OF MY SISTER'S CLUTCHES SO SHE CAN MEET HIM? WELL, IT WON'T BE EASY, BUT I'LL TRY!

I CAN ALREADY IMAGINE VANILLA'S FACE! **HA! HA!**
WHAT?! REALLY, I JUST WANTED...
WELL, ACTUALLY, INTRODUCING HIM TO NICKY IS MUCH BETTER THAN AN AUTOGRAPH!
OF COURSE, VIC'S COMPLETELY FLIPPED! HE ALWAYS MANAGES TO SURPRISE ME!
SMACK
THE NEXT MORNING, ON WINDY ISLAND...
HOW DO I LOOK, MOM?
YOU LOOK SCRUMPTIOUS, DAUGHTER! YOU'LL LEAVE OUR CHAMPION BREATHLESS!
GARY MOON, AUSTRALIAN SURFING CHAMPION, STEPS OUT OF THE AIRPLANE AND IS MOBBED BY PHOTOGRAPHERS!
TURN THIS WAY, GARY!
GIVE US YOUR IMPRESSIONS, GARY!
ACK!
FLASH
FLASH
FLASH
HEY! HOW RUDE!
IT'S REAL TORTURE FOR A SHY MOUSE LIKE HIM!
FLASH
OUCH! I'D RATHER FACE STORMY SEAS THAN THESE PAPARAZZI!

NOW CUT THAT OUT! LET HIM BREATHE!
???
WELCOME TO WINDY ISLAND, GARY!
THANKS, MISS...?
I'M VANILLA DE VISSEN!
THANKS, MISS VANILLA!
CLAP CLAP
A REAL STAR!
SHE'S SO LOVELY! AND WHAT A SPITFIRE!
CLAP CLAP
I'M JACK CAMERON, GARY MOON'S AGENT. I'M AT YOUR SERVICE, MS. DE VISSEN!
OH, IT'S JUST YOU!
IS IT CLEAR WHAT GARY IS SUPPOSED TO DO? I'M NOT JUST PAYING HIM TO STAR IN THE COMMERCIAL!
NO PROBLEM! HE DOES EVERYTHING I TELL HIM!
MY PUBLICITY TEAM SUGGESTED WE INVENT A LOVE STORY BETWEEN GARY AND MY DAUGHTER!
MY LITTLE ONE IS A FAN OF HIS, BUT... DON'T LET GARY GET THE WRONG IDEA!
DON'T WORRY, MA'AM... I REALLY DON'T THINK VANILLA IS HIS TYPE...
OF COURSE, SHE'LL BREAK GARY'S HEART! BUT I HAVE OTHER PROJECTS IN MIND FOR MY LITTLE CHEESE PUFF!
?!

THEY'VE GOT THE SET ALL READY TO GO! ALRIGHT, LET'S FILM RIGHT AWAY!
LET'S TAKE A WALK, JUST YOU AND ME! THE ISLAND'S SO ROMANTIC...
IT'S BEEN 24 HOURS SINCE I'VE BEEN IN THE WATER! STELLA'S VERY DEHYDRATED!
STELLA? WHO'S STELLA?
MY SURFBOARD! I CALL HER... STELLA!
HMPH...
IF VANILLA WANTS TO STAY AT THE CHAMP'S SIDE, SHE'LL HAVE TO PART WITH HER NICE CLOTHES AND... GET IN THE WATER!
FILM NOW? FINE WITH ME!
BRING ME MY SURF SUIT!
THE WATER'S FINE! HURRY UP, VANILLA!
OOF! THE WATER MUST BE FREEZING!
READY ON THE SET... ACTION!

FIRST, YOU CALMLY RIDE THE WAVES! THEN, WHEN A BIGGER WAVE COMES, YOU LET YOURSELF GET SWAMPED... AND GARY COMES TO SAVE YOU! GOT IT?

-GULP!- I'VE NEVER RIDDEN SUCH A BIG WAVE!

LOOSEN UP, VANILLA! DON'T BE AFRAID!

-GASP!-

SPLASH

HELPPP!

VANILLAAA!

HA! HA! HA! WHAT AN ARTIST!

OH, CUT IT OUT! DON'T BE JEALOUS OF YOUR SISTER!

ME, JEALOUS?! YOU'RE THE ONE WHO DOTES ON HER!

IN THE EVENING, THE LUXURIOUS ***SURF CLUB*** COMES ALIVE WITH GUESTS FOR THE OPENING...

WHAT LUXURY!

FLASH

FLASH

WHAT A MAGNIFICENT BUFFET!

WOW! SO MANY PEOPLE!

BUT WHERE'D THEY HIDE WONDERFUL GARY?

LOOK FOR VANILLA AND YOU'RE SURE TO FIND HIM...

COME ON, NICKY! DON'T BE SO SHY... HE'S JUST A GUY!

HEY, THERE! YOU FINALLY GOT HERE!

WHY? WERE YOU WAITING FOR US?

COME WITH ME, NICKY! VANILLA'S MOVED AWAY... WE HAVE TO TAKE ADVANTAGE OF IT!

HUH?!

HEY! WHERE'RE YOU TAKING HER?!

HEY! WATCH WHERE YOU'RE GOING!
HERE'S THE SOLUTION TO YOUR PROBLEM! HER NAME IS NICKY AND SHE'S A WHIRLWIND ON THE WAVES!
??
SHE CAN BE VANILLA'S STUNT DOUBLE!
PERFECT! THAT WAY, YOUR SISTER WILL STAY CALM AND DRY AND... THERE'LL BE NO MORE HYSTERICS!
PLEASED TO MEET YOU, NICKY!
M-ME, TOO! UM, I MEAN... I'M P-PLEASED, TOO... COUGH... I-I'M AUSTRALIAN, TOO!
A FELLOW SURFING COMPATRIOT! FANTASTIC!
YEAH!
R-RIGHT! F-FANTASTIC!
WHAT'D I TELL YOU? VIC'S NOT AS BAD AS HE SEEMS AFTER ALL! IT WAS A GOOD IDEA TO TALK TO HIM!
I'M SO THRILLED FOR NICKY!

STOP STARING AT THEM! LET'S DIVE INTO THE BUFFET!
BUT I WANT TO SEE...
IT'S A GALA EVENING AND AN EVENING OF SPECIAL ENCOUNTERS AT THE SURF CLUB...
MMM..., THESE CANAPÉS ARE DELICIOUS!
NOT AS DELICIOUS AS YOURS, MISS WHALE!
YOUR CHEESE CANAPÉS ARE PEARLS OF DELIGHT THAT GO FROM THE STOMACH STRAIGHT TO THE HEART!
OOOH! YOU FLATTER ME, MR. ROMEO!
AH, IF I COULD ONLY FIND THE COURAGE...
TO DO WHAT?
OH, HEAVENS! HE WANTS TO ASK FOR MY HAND IN MARRIAGE!
MISS WHALE! WOULD YOU BECOME... MY CHEF?
CH-CH-EF?!

CHEF! UMPH!
ERK?!

THE EVENING STILL HAS OTHER SURPRISES IN STORE!
NICKY!

WHAT'S **THAT GIRL** DOING WITH GARY?!
CALM DOWN, LITTLE SIS! EVERYTHING'S OKAY!

SHE'S SAVING YOU FROM THE WAVES, 'NILLA!
SHE'S GOING TO BE YOUR **STUNT DOUBLE** IN THE TOUGH SCENE! EVEN MOM AGREES!
YOU WERE THE ONE WHO INTRODUCED HIM TO HER, RIGHT?

GRRR... YOU SNAKE!
CRASH

MOM! YOU CAN'T ALLOW IT! IT'S NOT FAIR!
?

THEY WANT TO REPLACE ME IN THE COMMERCIAL! THEY GOT NICKY TO TAKE MY PLACE!
NO ONE IS REPLACING YOU, SWEETHEART! BUT THAT WAVE IS TOO DANGEROUS FOR YOU! THEY'LL JUST FILM YOU IN THE FOREGROUND!

ALL THE BIG STARS USE STUNT DOUBLES! DO YOU WANT TO BE LESS THAN THEM, PERHAPS?
HMM..

WHAT'S GOING ON, VANILLA?
WHY'S GARY TALKING TO NICKY?
SHE'S SO DULL...
!

NICKY'S GOING TO BE MY STUNT DOUBLE! ALL THE BIG STARS HAVE ONE... DON'T YOU KNOW?

COME ON, GARY... THE PHOTOGRAPHERS ARE CALLING FOR US!
AGAIN?

SEE YOU TOMORROW...
SEE YOU TOMORROW...
WELLLL!
JUST A STUNT DOUBLE, RIGHT?

THE NEXT DAY, NICKY AND GARY RIDE THE WAVES TOGETHER...
HE'S RESERVED: HE DOESN'T LIKE CROWDS AND ONLY FEELS AT EASE ON HIS SURFBOARD...
GARY♡
I'LL LEAD YOU, NICKY! TRUST ME!
... BUT IT DOESN'T TAKE MANY WORDS TO KNOW THEY BOTH LIKE THE SAME THINGS!
THANKS, VIC!
DON'T MENTION IT! AGGRAVATING VANILLA IS MY FAVORITE SPORT!
HMPH!
DON'T WORRY! KEEP IN MIND, YOU'LL BE GARY'S GUIDE FOR THE WHOLE DAY TOMORROW!
NO SCHOOL TOMORROW? OH, MOM, YOU'RE GREAT!
SMACK♡
I'VE PLANNED EVERYTHING, BECAUSE PAYING ATTENTION TO EVERY DETAIL LEADS TO PERFECTION! EVEN MY WAVES ARE WORKING WONDERFULLY!

BEAUTIFUL WAVES BUT... PERHAPS A BIT TOO BIG FOR A CALM DAY!
HELLO, ENGINEER O'CONNOR! DID YOU GET THE MEASUREMENTS FOR THE WINDY ISLAND REEF?
YES, PROFESSOR VAN KRAKEN. I GOT THEM BUT... THEY'RE ALL WRONG!
I ASSURE YOU, THEY'RE EXACT TO THE MILLIMETER!
IMPOSSIBLE! I DREW UP THE PLANS MYSELF... ALTHOUGH I DIDN'T WATCH THE CONSTRUCTION WORK AFTERWARDS.
THE MEASUREMENTS YOU SENT ARE ROUGHLY DOUBLE MINE!
OBVIOUSLY, THEY MODIFIED THE PLANS!
THAT'S ABSURD! INSANE! AN ARTIFICIAL REEF THAT BIG WILL CAUSE A DISASTER! WE MUST TEAR IT DOWN IMMEDIATELY!
UNDER THE STARRY SKY, THOSE DANGEROUS WAVES SEEM PERFECT TO NICKY AND GARY AFTER A DAY OF FILMING...
AND THIS MOMENT IN THEIR LIVES ALSO SEEMS PERFECT!
THAT SHOULD BE GARY AND ME! YOU'LL PAY FOR THIS, NICKY!

ON MONDAY MORNING, IT WAS HARD FOR NICKY TO GET BACK TO FOCUSING ON HER STUDIES...
AND EVEN GARY HAS HIS HEAD IN THE CLOUDS! HE LETS HIMSELF BE DRAGGED AROUND WHALE ISLAND, BUT HE DOESN'T SEE ANYTHING THAT'S GOING ON AROUND HIM!
SMILE FOR THE PHOTOGRAPHERS, GARY!
HUH? WHAT'D YOU SAY?
FLASH
VISSIA PLANNED OUT THE CHAMPION'S EVERY STEP...
GARY MOON! WELCOME TO WHALE ISLAND!
... IN AGREEMENT WITH JACK CAMERON, HIS AGENT!
Gary Moon
HURRAY FOR SURFING!
GARY, YOU'RE GREAT!
GARY
Gary

CLAP CLAP
CLAP CLAP
CLAP
IT'S GREAT! IT'LL BRING LOADS OF TOURISTS TO OUR ISLAND!
TO WINDY ISLAND, YOU MEAN!

TO OUR ISLAND TOO, IF WE BUILD A SURF CENTER!
I'M ***AGAINST*** THAT SURF CENTER AND THE ARTIFICIAL REEF! THE WAVES AT VERY WINDY POINT ARE ALREADY TOO BIG!

YOU FISHERMEN ARE AGAINST **PROGRESS!**
AND YOU SHOPKEEPERS ONLY THINK ABOUT **MONEY!**

STOP FIGHTING! THERE'S THE ***TV CREW!*** YOU'RE ON CAMERA!

HI, DINA! CAN YOU SEE ME?

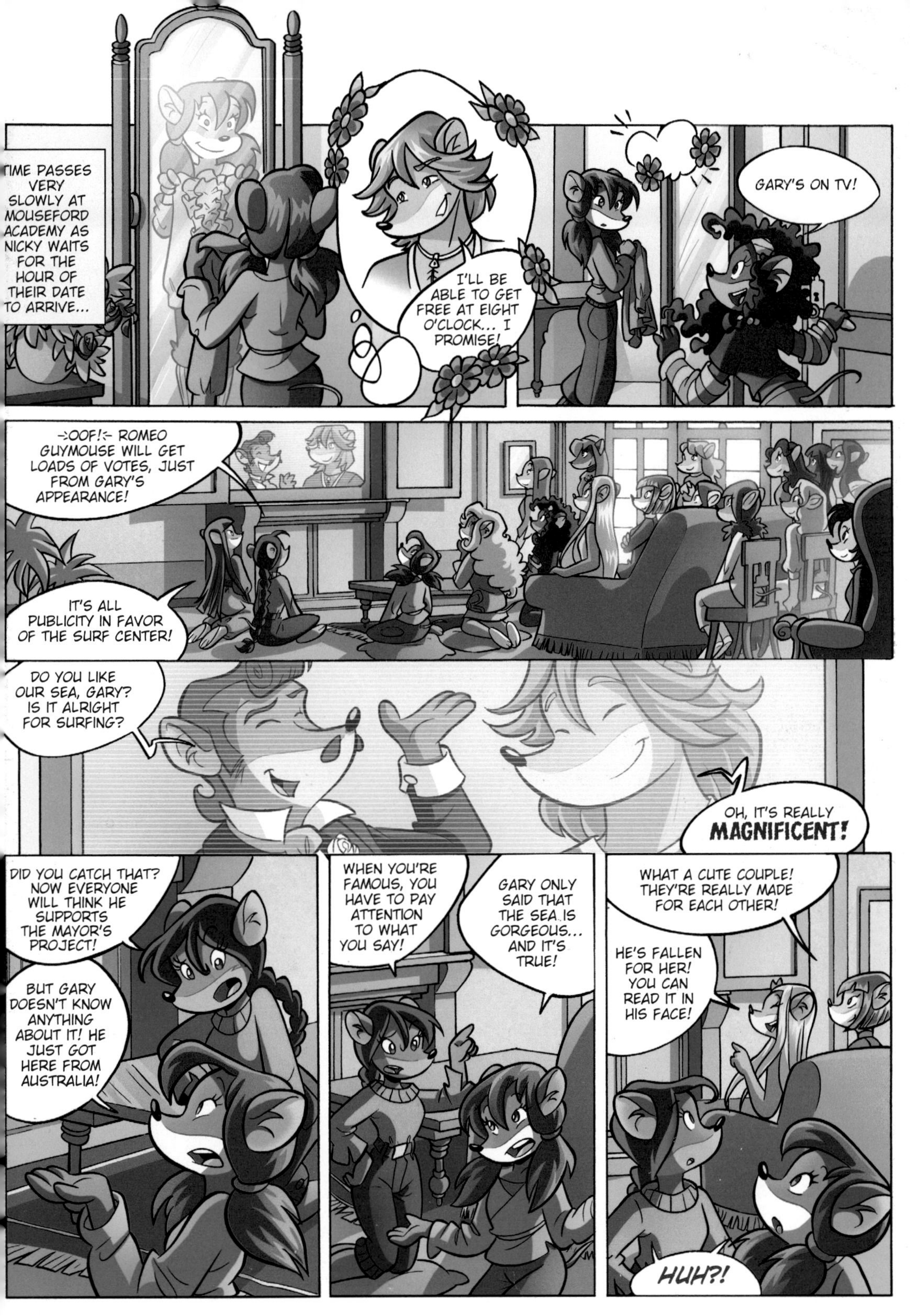
TIME PASSES VERY SLOWLY AT MOUSEFORD ACADEMY AS NICKY WAITS FOR THE HOUR OF THEIR DATE TO ARRIVE...
I'LL BE ABLE TO GET FREE AT EIGHT O'CLOCK... I PROMISE!
GARY'S ON TV!
–OOF!– ROMEO GUYMOUSE WILL GET LOADS OF VOTES, JUST FROM GARY'S APPEARANCE!
IT'S ALL PUBLICITY IN FAVOR OF THE SURF CENTER!
DO YOU LIKE OUR SEA, GARY? IS IT ALRIGHT FOR SURFING?
OH, IT'S REALLY MAGNIFICENT!
DID YOU CATCH THAT? NOW EVERYONE WILL THINK HE SUPPORTS THE MAYOR'S PROJECT!
BUT GARY DOESN'T KNOW ANYTHING ABOUT IT! HE JUST GOT HERE FROM AUSTRALIA!
WHEN YOU'RE FAMOUS, YOU HAVE TO PAY ATTENTION TO WHAT YOU SAY!
GARY ONLY SAID THAT THE SEA IS GORGEOUS... AND IT'S TRUE!
WHAT A CUTE COUPLE! THEY'RE REALLY MADE FOR EACH OTHER!
HE'S FALLEN FOR HER! YOU CAN READ IT IN HIS FACE!
HUH?!

SOME PICTURES HURT MORE THAN ANY WORDS...
!
... AND THEN THE TWO INDULGED THEMSELVES WITH A ROMANTIC BREAK AT CHEZ ROMEO!
HE'S BEEN PLAYING ME FOR A FOOL!
SOB!
NICKY!
I CAN'T WAIT TO TELL VANILLA ABOUT IT! HEE! HEE!
COME ON, OPEN UP!
KNOCK KNOCK
DON'T DO THIS, NICKY!
THERE MUST'VE BEEN A MISUNDERSTANDING!
LEAVE HER ALONE! SHE NEEDS TO LET OFF SOME STEAM!
WHAT A CAD!
CHAMPIONS ARE USED TO HAVING GIRLS THROW THEM-SELVES AT THEM!
THE THEA SISTERS ARE WRONG, BUT IT DOESN'T LOOK GOOD FOR GARY. SO...
NICKY'S NOT ANSWERING HER CELL PHONE! WHERE IS SHE? I DON'T UNDERSTAND! WHAT COULD HAVE HAPPENED?

NICKY'S NOT THE ONLY PERSON AT MOUSEFORD ACADEMY WHO FEELS BETRAYED...
NOW HE'S SENDING ME ROSES?! HE STILL HASN'T FIGURED OUT THAT I DON'T WANT TO BE HIS CHEF!
GIMME THAT!
OOPS!
WATCH AND TELL HIM EXACTLY WHAT MISS WHALE DID TO HIS ROSES!
BUT...
HA! HA! HA!
STOMP
STOMP
STOMP
THERE WE GO!
UM, REALLY...
...THE FLOWERS WERE FOR A CERTAIN MISS NICKY!
xNicky
GULP! OH, HEAVENS! WHAT KIND OF A MESS HAVE I MADE?
YOU HAVE TO FIX IT RIGHT AWAY! RUN! GET ANOTHER BOUQUET OF ROSES!
IT'S IMPOSSIBLE THIS EVENING! THE SHOP IS CLOSED!

THE NEXT MORNING, THE SKIES ARE COVERED WITH CLOUDS, JUST LIKE NICKY'S HEART...
WHY'D HE LEAD ME ON LIKE THAT?
AND LIKE GARY'S HEART...
SHE DIDN'T COME AND SHE DIDN'T CALL ME!
WOOSH
SPLASH
THE WIND IS BLOWING HARD AND THE WAVES ARE HUGE!
ARE YOU SURE YOU EVEN WANT TO GO IN THE WATER IN THIS WEATHER?
OF COURSE! TODAY'S THE PERFECT DAY FOR DOING STUNTS!
COME, QUICKLY! ROLL 'EM!
DON'T GET TOO FAR FROM THE SHORE, KID! SQUALLS COME ON SUDDENLY HERE!
NICKY CAN'T THINK OF ANYTHING EXCEPT HIM! BUT SHE DOESN'T WANT TO ADMIT IT, NOT EVEN TO HER CLOSEST FRIENDS!
I SHOULD HATE HIM, BUT INSTEAD... OH, GARY, I MISS YOU SO MUCH!
WHAT I WOULDN'T GIVE TO BE SURFING THE WAVES WITH YOU!

AROUND PEOPLE, HE FEELS AWKWARD. OTHER KIDS MAKE HIM FEEL INSECURE. BUT THE WAVES DON'T SCARE HIM AT ALL...
HE'S SO GOOD! IT'S AS IF HE'S BARELY SKIMMING THE SURFACE OF THE WATER!
GARY VENTS HIS FRUSTRATIONS ON THE CHALLENGES OF THE ROUGH SEAS!
ONLY ON HIS SURFBOARD DO ALL HIS DOUBTS DESERT HIM... AND HE SPREADS HIS WINGS!
OH, NO... THAT WAVE IS GIGANTIC! LOOK OUT, GARY!

IT SEEMS AS IF A MOUNTAIN IS RISING FROM THE SEA! IT'S A WAVE SO TALL THAT GARY CAN'T EVEN SEE THE END OF IT!
AAAGH!
GARYYYYY!
AN ENORMOUS WALL OF WATER COVERS GARY...
AHHH!
KRAAAASHHH
HEEEELP!
... AND THEN ANYTHING IN ITS PATH!
WOOOOSHH!

NICKY IS THE FIRST TO SOUND THE ALARM!
HELP! A WAVE..GARY... HELP!
??

WHAT'S HAPPENED, NICKY?
SLOW DOWN...
-:-SOB!-:-

A GIGANTIC WAVE SWAMPED GARY... -:-SOB-:-... AND THE BOATS AND EVERYTHING ELSE, TOO... -:-SOB!-:-

DID I HEAR YOU RIGHT? A WAVE DEMOLISHED WINDY ISLAND?
YES! WE HAVE TO HURRY AND HELP THE RESCUERS! RIGHT AWAY!

VIC'S FIRST THOUGHT IS OF HIS MOTHER...
HELLO? HELLO? MOM, ARE YOU OKAY?

OH, VIC, WHAT A TERRIBLE WAVE! IT SWEPT THROUGH THE CABANAS, THE BOATS... LUCKILY, ONLY THE FILM CREW WAS THERE!

ALARM SPREADS ACROSS ALL OF Whale Island...
IN THE FACE OF AN EMERGENCY, THEY ALL PUT ASIDE THEIR DIFFERENCES AND RUSH TO HELP WHOEVER'S AT SEA!
TOOT TOOT TOOOOooT

EVEN THE BIG MOUSEFORD ACADEMY MOTORBOAT JOINS THE VESSELS, WITH PROFESSOR VAN KRAKEN, VIOLET, COLETTE, AND NICKY ON BOARD...
... AND VIC JOINS IN ON HIS MOTORBOAT TOO, WITH PAMELA AND PAULINA ON BOARD!

NINE MICE ARE MISSING FROM WINDY ISLAND! BUT WITH THE ROUGH SEAS, IT'S NOT EASY TO LOCATE THEM!

DESPITE THE DIFFICULTY, EVERYONE IN THE WATER IS FISHED OUT, ONE AFTER ANOTHER!
SPLASH

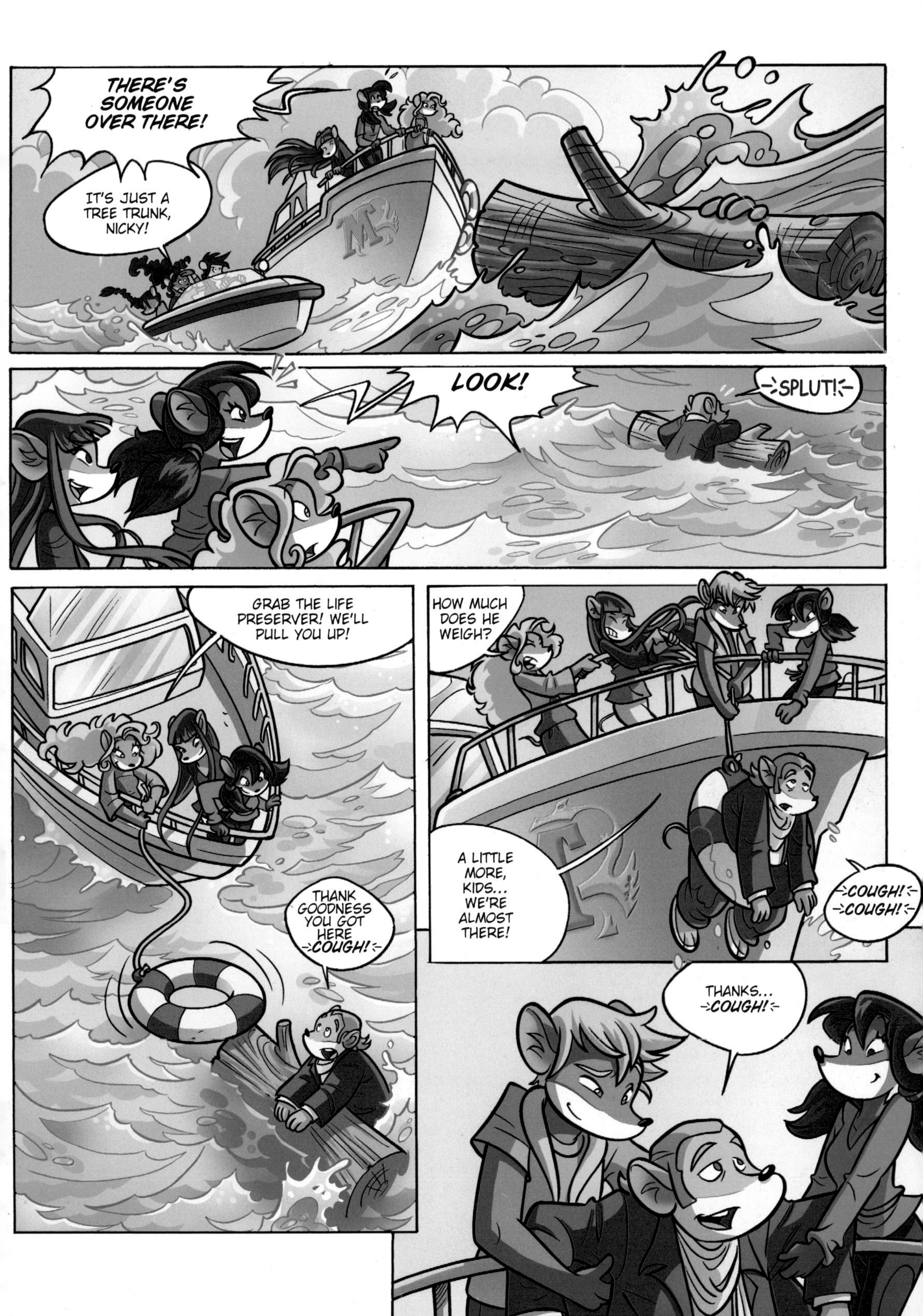
THERE'S SOMEONE OVER THERE!
IT'S JUST A TREE TRUNK, NICKY!
LOOK!
-SPLUT!-
GRAB THE LIFE PRESERVER! WE'LL PULL YOU UP!
THANK GOODNESS YOU GOT HERE -COUGH!-
HOW MUCH DOES HE WEIGH?
A LITTLE MORE, KIDS... WE'RE ALMOST THERE!
-COUGH! -COUGH!-
THANKS... -COUGH!-

WE FOUND THE DIRECTOR! IS ANYONE ELSE MISSING?
ONLY GARY MOON!
OH, NO!
"GARY WAS SWAMPED BY THE FIRST WAVE! HE MUST'VE BEEN DRAGGED OUT MUCH FARTHER THAN THE OTHERS!"
RNNN
RNNN
"LET'S EXPAND OUR SEARCH! WE SHOULD COVER A BIGGER AREA!"
WE'LL FIND HIM, YOU'LL SEE! GARY'S A CHAMP. HE'S GOT MUCH MORE STAMINA THAN THE REST OF US!
AND BESIDES, LOOK... THE SQUALL'S PASSED THROUGH! IT'LL BE EASIER TO SPOT HIM!
YOU'RE RIGHT! HE'S NEAR HERE... I CAN FEEL IT!

STILL, THE HOURS PASS AND THERE'S NO TRACE OF GARY...
TAKE A LITTLE BREAK, VIC! I CAN DRIVE YOUR MOTORBOAT!
THANKS, PAM! IS THERE STILL SOME TEA IN THE THERMOS?
IT'S THE LAST CUP! I'M AFRAID IT WON'T BE HOT ANY MORE BUT...
?
TURN RIGHT, PAM! I SAW SOMETHING ORANGE... LIKE GARY'S BOARD!
"YOU'RE RIGHT! IT'S REALLY HIM!"
RNNNNNN
GARY! GARY!
LOOK OUT, PAM! YOU'RE MAKING THE WAVES TOO BIG! THE BOARD'S TILTING!
MUSTY MOZZARELLA! HE'S UNCONSCIOUS.
BE CAREFUL, VIC! THE CURRENT'S VERY STRONG HERE!
I'LL LET THE OTHERS KNOW WE FOUND HIM!
SPLASH

I CAN FEEL HIS HEART BEATING!

PAMELA WAS RIGHT... THE CURRENT IS DRAGGING ME AWAY!

I CAN'T KEEP GOING! I'VE GOT TO TAKE A BREATH!

WHEN IS HE GOING TO RESURFACE?

I DON'T SEE ANYTHING...

OVER THERE!

WHEW!

RNNNNN

HANG ON THERE, VIC... HEEEEERE I COME!

FLASH

CLAP

CLAP CLAP

OOPS!

FLASH FLASH

CLAP CLAP

FLASH

CLAP CLAP

HURRAY!

THANKS, PAM! THANKS, PAULINA!
IT WAS VIC WHO DOVE IN AND FISHED GARY OUT! THE CURRENT ALMOST DRAGGED THEM AWAY!

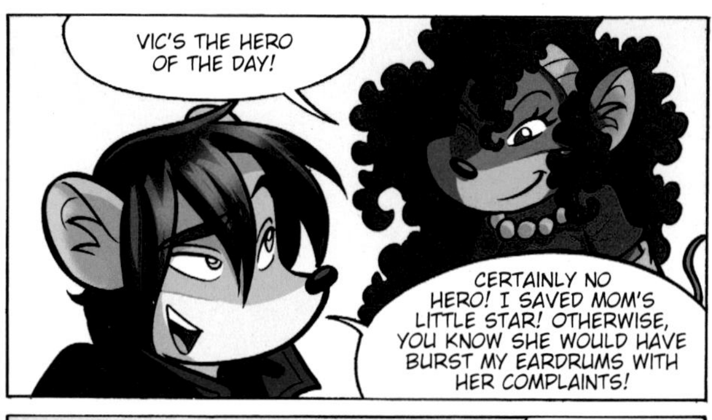
VIC'S THE HERO OF THE DAY!
CERTAINLY NO HERO! I SAVED MOM'S LITTLE STAR! OTHERWISE, YOU KNOW SHE WOULD HAVE BURST MY EARDRUMS WITH HER COMPLAINTS!

MAKE WAY! OUT OF THE WAY! I HAVE TO DELIVER THESE FLOWERS TO MISS NICKY!

ARE THEY FOR ME?
x Nicky

OH, GARY! YOU SENT THEM TO ME!
ME? YES, BUT... YOU WERE SUPPOSED TO DELIVER THEM YESTERDAY!

PHEW!
ON WHALE ISLAND, WE ALWAYS DELIVER FLOWERS AT... AHEM... JUST THE RIGHT TIME!
HEE! HEE! HEE!
PROBLEM SOLVED!

THE EVENT SHOULD HAVE BEEN A DISASTER FOR VISSIA, BUT INSTEAD...
NEWSPAPERS ALL OVER THE WORLD ARE TALKING ABOUT NOTHING ELSE!
ABOUT THE GIANT WAVE?
ABOUT THE LOVE STORY BETWEEN GARY AND HIS RESCUER!
JACK CAMERON CULTIVATED THE JOURNALISTS PROPERLY! HE'S CREATED A WHISKERFUL OF A LOVE STORY!
EXCELLENT! THAT WAY, NO ONE WILL THINK ABOUT THE GIANT WAVE AND THE DANGER WE FACED!
I'LL ADVERTISE MY ISLAND AS A... LOVE NEST!
ALL'S WELL THAT ENDS WELL... BUT NOT FOR EVERYONE!
GRRR! I SEE THEIR PICTURE EVERYWHERE!
GARY AND NICKY! NICKY AND GARY! CAN'T ANYONE TALK ABOUT ANYTHING ELSE?!
VANILLA JILTED!
GRUNT!

VISSIA, HOWEVER, HADN'T TAKEN GARY MOON AND THE THEA SISTERS INTO ACCOUNT...
PLEASE CHANGE YOUR MIND, GARY! DON'T DO IT!
IT'S USELESS TO INSIST, JACK... I'VE ALREADY DECIDED!

THE CONTRACT WITH MS. DE VISSEN MEANS NOTHING TO ME! AS FOR YOU... YOU'RE FIRED!
OH!

READY FOR THE PRESS CONFERENCE, GARY?
YES, OF COURSE, BUT...

...YOU'LL HELP ME, RIGHT? I'M A TOTAL WASHOUT WHEN I SPEAK IN PUBLIC!
THE THEA SISTERS AND PROFESSOR VAN KRAKEN WILL BE BY YOUR SIDE! AND MAYBE EVEN THEA STILTON, IF SHE GETS HERE IN TIME!

UM, HELLO, EVERYBODY! THANKS FOR COMING!
I'M NOT A GREAT SPEAKER, SO I'LL GET RIGHT TO THE POINT...

WHAT HAPPENED ON WINDY ISLAND WAS NOT AN ACCIDENT AT ALL!
IT WASN'T AN ACCIDENT?
WHAT WAS IT?! HOW DO YOU EXPLAIN THAT GIGANTIC WAVE?

IT WAS CAUSED BY THE ARTIFICIAL REEF! UM... MY FRIENDS WILL EXPLAIN IT BETTER THAN I CAN!

THE ARTIFICIAL REEF THAT VISSIA DE VISSEN BUILT IS TOO BIG! WHEN THE WINDS ARE STRONG, IT CREATES UNCONTROL-LABLE WAVES!

DO YOU HAVE PROOF OF WHAT YOU'RE CLAIMING?
OF COURSE! I HAVE A SWORN AFFIDAVIT FROM ENGINEER O'CONNOR, WHO DESIGNED THE REEF! I CAN READ IT TO YOU...

NO NEED FOR THE AFFIDAVIT, PROFESSOR! WE HAVE ENGINEER O'CONNOR HERE IN PERSON!
THEA STILTON?!
SHE DID IT! SHE GOT HERE IN TIME!
THEA!

ONE OF YOUR USUAL SCOOPS, THEA?
NO! I JUST CONVINCED ENGINEER O'CONNOR TO CATCH THE FIRST PLANE OUT OF SCOTLAND... SO HE COULD ANSWER YOUR QUESTIONS!

THEY GOT THE SCOOP THEMSELVES... THE THEA SISTERS! MY PROTÉGÉS!

I'D LIKE TO INTRODUCE GARY MOON TO YOU, THEA!
PLEASED TO MEET YOU, CHAMP!
THE PLEASURE'S ALL MINE!
THANK YOU FOR COMING, MR. O'CONNOR!
IT WAS MY OBLIGATION, PROFESSOR! THAT REEF ABSOLUTELY MUST BE DEMOLISHED!

AND SO, AFTER A FULL EXPLANATION OF THE FACTS...
THEY'RE RIGHT!
THAT REEF IS DANGEROUS!
I'LL WRITE AN ARTICLE RIGHT AWAY!

THEN WE'RE IN AGREEMENT! WE'LL PUT YOUR STATEMENT ON PRIME TIME TV!
YOU CAN'T DO BETTER THAN THAT!
WE MUST INFORM THE WHALE ISLAND RESIDENTS ABOUT THE RISKS BEFORE THEY GO TO VOTE!

THE **WAVE** DIDN'T DEVASTATE JUST VISSIA'S ISLAND, BUT ALSO ROMEO GUYMOUSE'S REFERENDUM!
AND IF THAT WERE TO HAPPEN HERE?
A WAVE LIKE THAT WOULD BE ***DISASTROUS!***
YOU CAN'T PLAY AROUND WITH THE SEA! WE FISHERMEN KNOW THAT VERY WELL!

I HEARD MS. DE VISSEN WILL DEMOLISH HER REEF!
NOT DEMOLISH, JUST DIMINISH!

VOTING DAY FINALLY ARRIVES...
A MONSTROSITY LIKE THAT NEAR DONKEY ISLAND? NEVER, NEVER!
YOU'RE RIGHT! NO ARTIFICIAL REEFS FOR OUR ISLAND!

DID I GET HERE TOO LATE? HAVE THEY ALREADY ANNOUNCED THE RESULTS OF THE REFERENDUM?
NOT YET...
SHHH! HERE IT IS!

100% NO
MY DEAR TV VIEWERS, IT'S INCREDIBLE! THE RESULTS WERE UNANIMOUS!
EVERYONE VOTED NO! NOT A SINGLE CITIZEN OF WHALE ISLAND VOTED IN FAVOR OF THE REEF!

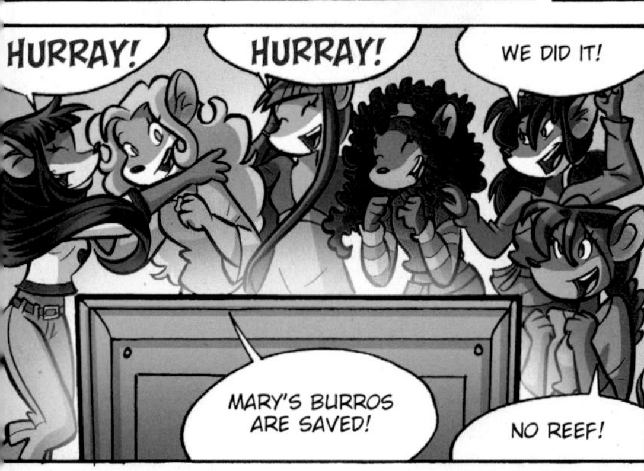
HURRAY!
HURRAY!
WE DID IT!
MARY'S BURROS ARE SAVED!
NO REEF!

HEY, IF EVERYONE VOTED "NO," THAT MEANS...
... EVEN THE MAYOR VOTED AGAINST HIS OWN PROPOSAL!

WHAT'D I TELL YOU? UNDERNEATH IT ALL, ROMEO ISN'T BAD! HE REALIZED HE WAS WRONG, IN THE END!
HA! HA! HA!
HEE! HEE! HEE!
AND THEREFORE... HURRAY FOR ROMEO GUYMOUSE!

THE TIME HAS COME FOR GARY TO LEAVE...
THEY'LL HAVE TO KEEP IN TOUCH WITH EACH OTHER LONG-DISTANCE...
BUT THEIR FEELINGS ARE STRONG! PLUS, THEY'VE DISCOVERED THEY HAVE ANOTHER POWERFUL BOND, IN ADDITION TO THEIR LOVE FOR SURFING AND AUSTRALIA...
... A COMMITMENT TO PROTECTING NATURE!
THE END

Watch Out For PAPERCUTZ™

Surf's up!

Welcome to the fabulous, fast-paced fourth THEA STILTON graphic novel from Papercutz, the fantastic folks dedicated to publishing great graphic novels for all ages. I'm Salicrup, *Jim Salicrup* Editor-in-Chief and unofficial Whale Island lifeguard.

While I may be a fan of Brian Wilson (of the Beach Boys) and surf music in general, I've never been all that interested in actually surfing—other than surfing the net, that is. I even loved all those great teenagers-at-the-beach movies from the 50s and 60s, especially the ones with Don Rickles or Buster Keaton. But unlike our body-surfing, Coney Island-haunting, letterer and production whiz, Big Bird Zatryb, I simply prefer to stay on dry land, preferably, the non-sandy kind. I'm more like my fellow Editor-in-Chief Geronimo Stilton that way, although he proved to be better than he even imagined when he competed in the 100-meter Swim in GERONIMO STILTON #10 "Geronimo Stilton Saves the Olympics"...

...MAYBE IF I PUT ALL MY ENERGY INTO THIS, I CAN STILL DO IT!

Even the stars of another Papercutz title, love to surf...

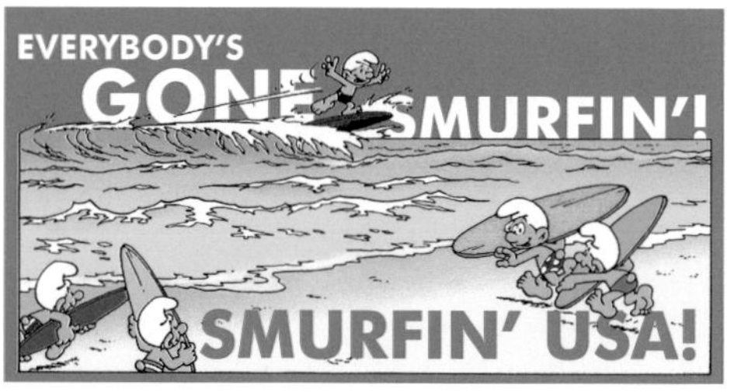
EVERYBODY'S GONE SMURFIN'!
SMURFIN' USA!

Yes, even Smurfs surf! Just check out "Smurf Surfing" in THE SMURFS #17 "The Strange Awakening of Lazy Smurf"!

And as we now know, Nicky, Pamela, and Paulina of the Thea Sisters, and even Vanilla de Vissen, surf too. So, while the odds are that you'll never catch me hangin' ten, that doesn't mean I don't enjoy stories about surfing. And "Catching the Giant Wave" was certainly an enjoyable tale, featuring a whole lot of surfing fun, fun, fun under the sun.

So until THEA STILTON #5, I simply leave you with the two words Nicky said over the phone to her new sweetie, the Australian surf champion, before he went to bed, "Goodnight, Moon!" (Sorry, I couldn't resist!)

Class dismissed!

Thanks,

JIM

Stay in Touch!

EMAIL:	salicrup@papercutz.com
WEB:	papercutz.com
TWITTER:	@papercutzgn
FACEBOOK:	PAPERCUTZGRAPHICNOVELS
FAN MAIL:	Papercutz, 160 Broadway, Suite 700, East Wing, New York, NY 10038

Special Preview of GERONIMO STILTON #15 "All for Stilton, Stilton for All!"

TRAP, CAN YOU REMIND ME WHY YOU'RE THE PILOT OF THIS HELICOPTER?
WELL, YOU ASKED THE PAPER FOR A SEASONED PILOT FOR A RECONNAISSANCE FLIGHT, AND HERE I AM!

UNCLE, YOU STILL HAVEN'T TOLD US WHY WE'RE HERE! WHY ALL THE URGENCY?

DURING THE LAST FEW WEEKS, THERE'VE BEEN SOME MYSTERIOUS SIGHTINGS AT THE LAKE. I WANT TO GET TO THE BOTTOM OF THIS!
MYSTERIOUS IN WHAT WAY?
OH, IT'S HARD TO EXPLAIN...

...REPORTS OF SUDDEN MOVEMENTS ON THE SURFACE OF THE LAKE...
...AND EVEN FRIGHTFUL SHAPES THAT VANISH INTO NOTHING SHORTLY AFTERWARDS.

DO YOU THINK THERE MIGHT BE A MONSTER AT LAGO-LAGO?
ABSOLUTELY NOT! THERE HAS TO BE A SCIENTIFIC EXPLANATION...

...AND WE'RE GOING TO FIND IT!

HERE WE ARE: THIS IS WHERE THE PREVIOUS SIGHTINGS WERE AT THIS TIME OF DAY!
THIS FOG SURE DOESN'T HELP MUCH...

I THINK I SEE SOMETHING OVER THERE. LET'S GO!

KEEP GOING THAT WAY...

I THINK I SEE...

LOOK OUT!

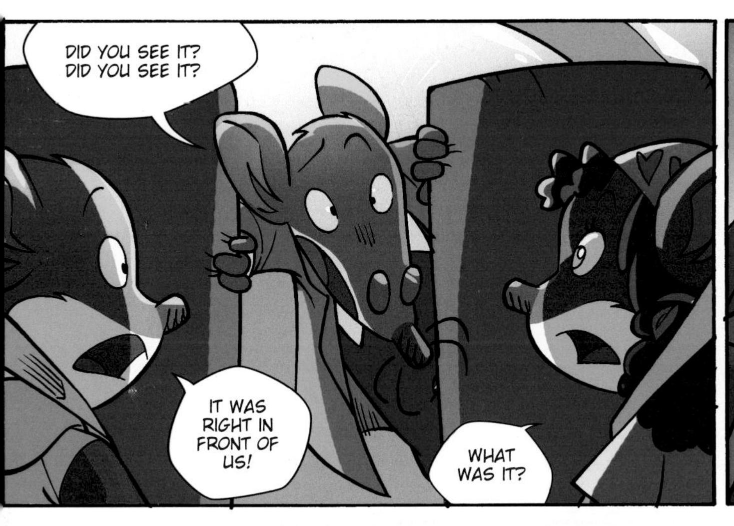
DID YOU SEE IT? DID YOU SEE IT?
IT WAS RIGHT IN FRONT OF US!
WHAT WAS IT?

I DON'T KNOW, BUT WE'RE ABOUT TO FIND OUT!

VRRMMMMMMMMM

YIKES! TRAP, WHAT ARE YOU DOING?
YOU SAID YOU WANTED TO GET TO THE BOTTOM OF THIS, AND NO ONE ESCAPES **TRAP THE PILOT!**

THERE IT IS! I SEE IT!

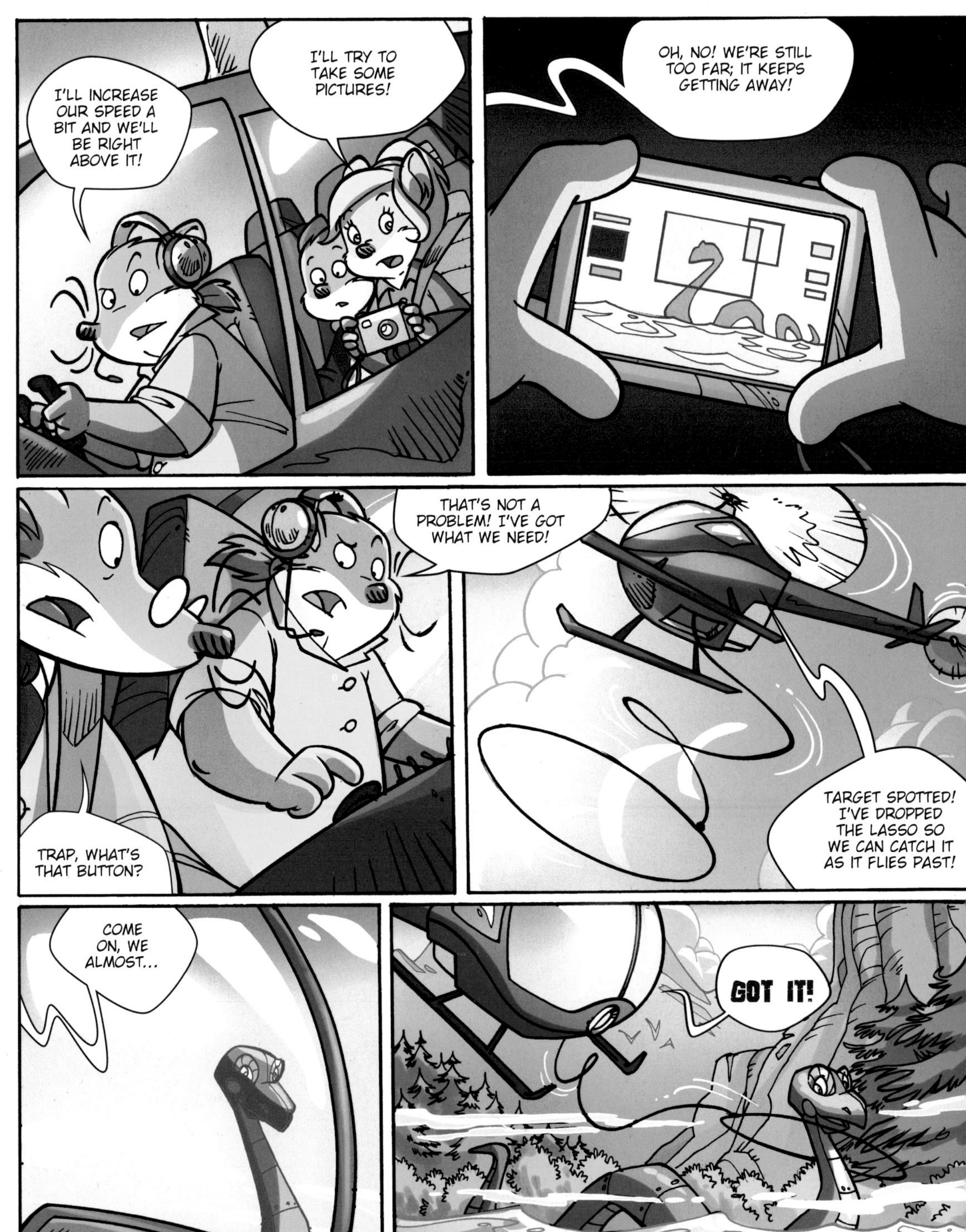

Don't Miss GERONIMO STILTON #15 "All for Stilton, Stilton for All!"

Hi, I'm Thea, special correspondent to the Rodent's Gazette, the most famouse paper on Mouse Island! I teach journalism at Mouseford Academy, where I've gotten to know five very special students! They're top-notch kids who've developed a real friendship for each other. They formed a group that they named after me: the Thea Sisters. I've decided to tell you about their adventures at Mouseford Academy: you'll have a blast!

Nicky is very brave: she's not afraid of anyone! Her only fear is enclosed spaces.

Pamela can be a bit grouchy, but she always goes out of her way to help her friends.

COLETTE loves gossip and remembers almost everything! Even unnecessary information might turn out to be useful!